W9-BFS-037

Max the Missing Puppy

Max the Missing Puppy

Holly Webb

Illustrated by Sophy Williams

For Rosie

STRIPES PUBLISHING
An imprint of Magi Publications
1 The Coda Centre, 189 Munster Road,
London SW6 6AW

A paperback original
First published in Great Britain in 2008
This edition published 2011

Text copyright © Holly Webb, 2008
Illustrations copyright © Sophy Williams, 2008

ISBN: 978-1-84715-210-7

The right of Holly Webb and Sophy Williams to be
identified as the author and illustrator of this work
respectively has been asserted by them in accordance
with the Copyright, Designs and Patents Act, 1988.

All rights reserved.

This book is sold subject to the condition that it shall not,
by way of trade or otherwise, be lent, resold, hired out, or
otherwise circulated without the publisher's prior consent
in any form of binding or cover other than that in which it
is published and without a similar condition, including this
condition, being imposed upon the subsequent purchaser.

A CIP catalogue record for this book is available
from the British Library.

Printed and bound in China.

STP/1800/0008/0911

10 9 8 7 6 5 4 3 2 1

Chapter One

Molly opened the gate, and stood holding it, waiting impatiently for her parents to catch up. "This is it!" she called. "Number forty-two!" She was sure she could hear squeaking and yapping from inside the house, and she couldn't wait to get inside.

At last her parents caught up. "Go on and ring the bell!" said Molly's dad.

Molly heard the bell chime inside the house, and it was followed by an explosion of deep woofs. Then she heard paws thudding, and claws clicking, and something thumped into the door. Molly jumped back in surprise.

"Jackson, get away! How can I open the door with you in front of it?" The voice didn't sound annoyed, more as though the dog's owner was trying not to laugh. "The rest of you aren't helping!"

The deep barking had now been joined by a lot of squeaky little noises, all sounding very excited. The door opened, and a friendly-looking woman attempted to hold back a tide of black and white puppies as they surged around her feet. An enormous gray, shaggy dog was sitting beside her.

"Oh, good, you shut the gate. The puppies are a bit excited, I'm afraid, and they're desperate to get out and explore. I'm Sally Hughes, we spoke on the phone. Come on in!"

"I'm James Martin," Molly's dad said, picking up a puppy who'd managed to scramble over Mrs. Hughes's foot. "You spoke to my wife Clare on the phone, and this is our daughter Molly. The dog-crazy one!"

They followed the excited puppies into the house. Molly looked at them in amazement. Mrs. Hughes had told her mom that there were six puppies, but surely there were more than six here? They seemed to be everywhere!

Mrs. Hughes led them into the kitchen and put the kettle on. Another giant dog was stretched out dozing on a comfy-looking cushion in the corner. Molly was sure she heard her groan as the puppies flooded back in and threw themselves all over her.

Mrs. Hughes smiled. "Poor Silkie! I think she's actually looking forward to the puppies going. She's a great mom, but they're wearing her out!" She put cups of coffee down in front of Molly's mom and dad, and poured Molly a glass of juice.

Molly sipped from her glass, perched on the edge of her chair, wishing she could go and play with the puppies who were still bouncing all over their mom.

Mrs. Hughes noticed her hopeful eyes and beamed at her. "Go on, get down and play with them! Just watch out for Jackson, the puppies' dad, he's completely friendly, but he's huge, and if he wants to join in he can knock you over without meaning to!"

Molly knelt down on the floor, and the puppies looked at her with interest. The bravest of them started to creep slowly over to her, tail wagging gently. Molly stretched out a hand hopefully, and he butted it with his soft little head, then darted back. Molly thought he looked almost as though he was giggling!

"Mrs. Hughes?" she asked, looking around. "Why don't the puppies look like Jackson and Silkie? They've got short fur, and they're black and white, but their parents are gray."

"That's the way it is with Old English sheepdogs," Mrs. Hughes explained.

"They're born with that short, springy black-and-white fur, and when it grows longer, it gets much lighter."

Dad was looking thoughtfully at Silkie, her long fur glossy and smooth as it trailed over her cushion. "It's going to be a lot of work, grooming."

Mrs. Hughes nodded seriously. "Yes, it really is. You have to make sure their coats are clean, and that they haven't got any sore patches under all that fur. And they need a *lot* of exercise. Old English sheepdogs are a big commitment. I mean, no dogs are easy to look after, but one of these can be hard work."

Molly looked up at her parents. It sounded scary, but she still wanted to take one of the puppies home!

Her mom was looking doubtful. "Maybe this isn't such a good idea, we've never had a dog before. Perhaps something smaller would be better…"

The bravest puppy, who had a mostly white face, with cute black ears, and a pirate-style eyepatch, was creeping up to Molly again. This time he jumped up so his paws were on her lap, and gave her a quick little lick.

Molly gasped delightedly. She'd been listening to her mom and hadn't noticed him. She tickled him under the chin. "I don't mind it being hard work," she said earnestly.

Another puppy, who had just the same gorgeous pirate look, bounded over and jumped into Molly's lap. Then he sat with his tongue hanging out, looking very pleased with himself.

Mrs. Hughes smiled. "It's not all work. They're incredibly affectionate dogs, and very playful and good with children. Your daughter will have a friend for life." She crouched down next to Molly. "Those two are the boy puppies, they're a real pair of rascals; they get into everything. The girls are a little bit more shy."

But now that their brothers had proved that this girl wasn't scary, the other puppies came crowding around to be stroked and petted too. Soon Molly was covered in a heaving black-and-white puppy blanket. She caught sight of Silkie watching her, one big dark eye peering out from behind her gorgeous long fringe. The big dog sighed happily, and Molly was sure she was glad that someone else was being climbed on for once.

Molly's parents had been talking quietly. Molly tried to listen, but the puppies kept licking her ears, which made it a bit tricky. She hoped they hadn't changed their minds! When they'd spotted the advertisement in the local paper saying *Puppies for Sale*, and seen that the house was only half an hour's drive away, it had seemed so perfect. It had taken forever to persuade Mom and Dad that she was old enough to have a dog. They'd been saying, "When you're older," for years! Molly didn't think she could bear it if she had to wait any longer. These puppies were so cute, and Jackson and Silkie were beautiful. Molly could just imagine running along the beach after school every day with a huge silvery-furred dog like Jackson galloping beside her.

At last Dad came over and squatted down next to the puppies too. Molly and all the puppies stared seriously at him. Then one of the bouncy boy puppies leaned over and whacked him on the arm with his head, looking up at him with twinkly dark eyes.

Dad gently picked up the puppy, and smiled over at Molly. "So, you think you can manage to keep one of these little rascals exercised?" he asked.

Molly gasped in delight. "You mean yes? We can have one?" She wrapped her arms around the other boy puppy, who was trying to burrow under her sweater.

"Yes. But you'll have to look after the puppy, Molly. And it won't be a puppy for that long, either—soon it will be a great big dog the size of Silkie and Jackson over there." Dad tickled his puppy, who wriggled happily. Then he looked down at the puppies romping all around them. "Now we just have to choose one…"

One!

Molly knew she ought to be over the moon about having a puppy at all, but she hadn't imagined quite how difficult it would be to pick just one. The puppies were all so sweet she wanted to take every one of them home! How could she choose one—when it meant leaving all the others behind?

The two cheeky boy puppies were scrapping over a chew-toy now, pulling it to and fro with mock-fierce growls. The fight looked even funnier because they were so alike, the same size and with almost identical markings. The only noticeable difference was that their eyepatches were on the opposite eyes—sitting side by side they were like mirror images.

"You like those two, don't you, Molly?" Mom asked, watching them and laughing as one of the puppies let go, leaving his brother rolling onto his bottom, still clutching the toy. "Shall we have one of the boys?"

"Oh yes, they're really sweet. But they both are, Mom, how are we going to choose just one of them?" Molly stretched out her fingers to the puppies, who came over at once to sniff and lick them. She tickled them behind their ears, and hugged them as they climbed up into her lap. "Couldn't we…?"

"Only one, Molly!" Mom said firmly. "One dog is quite enough work."

Dad was nodding too, and Molly sighed and looked back at the puppies. Just then, the puppy with the right eyepatch struggled off her knee and went to join his sisters, who were taking turns hanging off their mom's ears.

The other puppy watched them for a minute, then turned and gazed up at Molly, his tongue hanging out a bit so he looked gorgeously goofy. Molly giggled. "OK," she said, lifting him gently under his front legs, and snuggling him up against her shoulder.

"Please can we have this one? He's really friendly and cuddly."

Mom leaned over to pet him. "He definitely is adorable. What are we going to call him?"

Molly gave the puppy a thoughtful look as he slobbered into her shoulder. "I think we should call him Max!"

Chapter Two

A week later, Molly and her parents were able to take Max home. He was eight weeks old now, and ready to leave his mother. Two of his sisters were about to go to new homes too, and Mrs. Hughes said she was sure the others would find owners soon.

Molly still wished they could have Max's brother as well, they were such a matching pair that Molly hated to split them up. Then Max spotted Molly, flung himself at her, and nearly knocked her over, and Molly thought that maybe *two* dogs doing that all the time might be a bit much. But she was so happy that he remembered her!

"Hmmm. We're going to have to take him to a good puppy-training class," Molly's mom said. "It won't be long before he's big enough to hurt someone by accident. We need to be able to get him to calm down."

Mrs. Hughes was nodding. "I can recommend a trainer near you. Max's just had his first shots, so you can take him to classes in a couple of weeks when he's had the second set. It's really good to start young."

It was very exciting taking Max home, there was so much to show him. Mom and Dad had already spent ages fitting a dog-guard in the trunk of the car so that Max had his own special place to ride. Mom had to keep telling Molly to sit still, as she just couldn't help twisting around in her seat to check that Max was OK, all on his own back there.

At the house there was his new basket, his food bowl, and his leash for walks. Mrs. Hughes had said to introduce him to outdoor walks gently, as he was only used to quick runs in her backyard at the moment. Molly was really looking forward to taking him for walks on the beach, but they needed to wait until after Max's booster vaccinations.

Meanwhile Max was loving settling in to his new home. He did miss his brother and sisters, but Molly was a new and interesting person to play with, and he had her all to himself. He didn't have to share his toys either, and there were so many! Molly had spent all her allowance on tennis balls, and a hard nylon bone that would be good for Max's new teeth. They had a great afternoon, playing new and exciting games. Max ran around so much he fell asleep in the middle of a game of peekaboo that they'd invented with the blanket from his basket. He suddenly stopped bouncing, and when

Molly peered worriedly under the blanket to check he was all right, she found him laid out with his nose between his paws, fast asleep.

Molly had begged for Max to be allowed to sleep in her room, but Mom and Dad said no. They knew it would end up with Max on Molly's bed and not in his basket, even though Molly promised it wouldn't. "It's all very well having a puppy on your bed, Molly," Mom explained, "but once Max is his full size, there'd be no room in your bed for you! You can't let him onto your bed now and then change your mind when he's bigger, he wouldn't understand."

So Max had to stay downstairs. Molly had given him her old teddy bear to snuggle up to, and a hot-water bottle, so he'd feel like he was curled up next to his mom, but it wasn't the same. After all the cuddles and fussing, Max didn't understand why he was suddenly all on his own. He yapped hopefully, expecting someone to come back and play with him, but no one came. He got up, and pattered around the kitchen sniffing, trying to work out where they all were. Earlier on Molly had played a game where she popped out from behind chairs at him—maybe this was the same? But she wasn't behind any of the chairs.

Max trailed back to his basket with his tail hanging sadly. Where had they all gone? Were they going to come back? He snuffled and whimpered to himself for a little while, then the exhausting day caught up with him again, and he fell asleep, burrowed into his blanket.

Upstairs Molly listened worriedly. It was so horrible hearing him cry, but Mom and Dad had explained that it would only upset Max more if she went down and then left him again. Her bedroom door was open, and she could hear the noises from the kitchen. She crept out very quietly, and leaned over the banisters. He sounded so sad! But he was definitely getting quieter, so perhaps he was going to sleep. Molly was tired herself from all the chasing around they'd been doing, so she sat down on the top step, leaning against the wall, and tried not to let her eyes close.

Molly's parents had been watching TV in the living room. When they came upstairs a couple of hours later, Molly was fast asleep on the top step.

"Max..." she muttered sleepily, as her dad lifted her.

"He's fast asleep in his bed, Molly, don't worry. Go to sleep."

The weekend just flew by. Back at school on Monday everyone was really envious when Molly told them about Max. She had a couple of photos that Dad had printed out for her, and she showed them off proudly.

"Oh, he's cute, Molly! My brother has an Old English sheepdog, they make great pets." Mrs. Ford, Molly's class teacher, looked at the photo admiringly as they stood in the playground before school. "You should show those to the class when we do show-and-tell."

Molly didn't normally like the class sharing sessions that much, as she never felt like she had anything very exciting to say! But today she couldn't wait to tell everyone about her puppy.

It was nice to have them all admiring Max's picture too, as she was really missing him. She couldn't help wondering what he was doing, and if he was missing her too. Mom had promised to make lots of fuss of Max, but she'd be busy doing stuff on the computer too, as she worked from home. Molly hoped she wouldn't get carried away and forget about him.

Molly's school was really close to her house, so she walked there with her mom, and they picked up her friend Amy, who lived three doors down, on the way. Then Amy's mom brought them home. That Monday, Molly hurried Amy all the way back to their street, and then she raced home and flung herself through the front door.

Max jumped up and shot out of the kitchen to greet her. He'd been curled up in his basket, half-dozing, and wishing someone would play with him. He loved his new house, but it got very quiet without Molly there. Molly's mom had tried her best, but she just wasn't the same. With Molly he didn't have to stand there holding his bone looking hopeful, she *knew* when he wanted to play. He danced around her, barking excitedly, and scrabbling at her knees. When she swept him up for a hug he did his best to lick her all over, wanting her to know how much he'd longed for her to come home.

"Ooooh, get off, get off, Max, not my ears, you're really tickling!" Molly held him out at arm's length and laughed at him. "I don't need washing, anyway. Did you have a nice day? Was he OK, Mom? Did he behave himself?"

Her mom was leaning on the door frame and laughing. "Yes, but I think he really missed you. He looked all around the house several times, and he sat by the front door for ages. Why don't you take him in the backyard for a run around? I took him out quickly at lunchtime, but I'm sure he'd like to go out again."

Max seemed to understand what "backyard" meant. He dashed to the door, and jumped up and down, squeaking.

Molly giggled. "No, I think I need a rest after school … it's OK, Max, I'm teasing! Come on, silly." She grabbed his squeaky ball and opened the door, letting Max streak out in a black-and-white blur.

He loved to be outside!

Max settled in very quickly, but he didn't stop missing Molly while she was at school—and she seemed to have to go to school all the time! He spent lots of time sniffing about for her, and he worked out that he could sneakily climb onto the back of the sofa to look out of the window and see if she was coming. He got yelled at if Molly's mom caught him doing that, though.

Max was sure that if only he could get outside, he could go and find Molly, and be with her. He knew she missed him too, and he didn't understand why she went out without him. It had only taken him a few days of being in the house without her to explore everywhere indoors. By the fifth day of Molly being at school, he was very bored.

"We'll play in the backyard all weekend, Max," Molly promised as she got ready to leave for school on Friday morning. "I really wish we could go on the beach, and show you the sea, but Mrs. Hughes said you'll have to wait until about a week after your second vaccinations."

"He'd probably only try and eat the sand," Mom said, looking at Max's food bowl. It was empty, as usual, and polished sparkly-clean. "That dog is always hungry." She scratched him under the chin to show she wasn't really angry, and Max closed his eyes and snuffled happily. It was his absolute favorite place to be tickled, and Mom and Molly sounded happy and excited. Everything was good.

Except Molly was about to go! Not again. Max gave a mournful little howl.

"I know, I'm sorry. But I'll be back this afternoon, and then we've got the whole weekend. And it's vacation! I'd almost forgotten! Nine days of no school. We'll spend loads of time outside, it's going to be brilliant." Molly kissed the top of his head, and followed Mom outside, leaving Max staring sadly at the door.

Molly's mom was very busy that day. She kept shooing Max away when he tried to play. She did take him for a couple of little runs in the backyard, but she wanted to go back in long before he did. By the middle of the afternoon, Max was really missing Molly. It was a hot, sleepy sort of day, even though it was only May, and being stuck in the house was making Max restless. Perhaps Molly's mom was ready to play again? Hopefully, he brought his squeaky bone to her for a game, but she said, "Not now, Max," in a really firm voice, so he went and lay down in his basket, feeling bored. He rested his chin on the edge of the basket and sighed. Maybe he should just have a sleep, and see if Molly's mom wanted to play later. His eyes were slowly closing when something fluttered past his nose. Max opened one eye to see a large butterfly swooping around his head. Surprised, he jumped up and barked furiously. What was it?

Mom dashed in, looking worried. Then she laughed. "Oh, Max, it's all right, it's only a butterfly. We'll send him out, don't panic. I suppose you've never seen one before."

The butterfly was in no hurry to leave. Mom tried to waft it back toward the kitchen window where it had come in, but it fluttered off into the living room, and eventually settled on the curtains. Mom opened the window and after a couple of failed attempts, she scooped it out with a magazine.

"There," she said, soothingly, putting the magazine back on the coffee table. "It's gone now. Oh, look, it's not long until Molly gets home. I have to go and finish a little bit of work." She went back to the computer in her office down the hall.

Max pricked up his ears when Mom mentioned Molly. Was she coming? He went and looked hopefully at the front door, but no Molly appeared. Disappointed, he wandered back into the living room and scrambled up onto the sofa so that he could look out of the window and wait for her.

Then he noticed that Mom had left the window open.

Max jumped up, and stuck his head out of the window, his nose quivering with excitement.

Now he could go and find Molly!

Molly dashed down the street from Amy's house, calling a quick good-bye over her shoulder. She let herself in the front door, panting, and expecting Max to be there leaping around her feet like a mad thing. But the house was strangely quiet. He must be asleep.

Molly headed quietly into the kitchen, not wanting to wake him. He was so cute when he was asleep. Max's basket was empty, and she looked around the kitchen, confused. Maybe he was sitting with Mom in her office?

Feeling a little anxious, Molly walked quickly back into the hallway and opened the office door.

Her mom looked up with a start. "Molly! I'm sorry, I didn't hear you come back. I've been desperately trying to get this finished before the vacation starts. Did you have a nice day?"

"Yes—but Mom, where's Max?"

Mom looked down at Molly's feet, as though she expected to see Max there. "Isn't he in his bed? I thought he was sleeping."

"No, I can't find him anywhere," Molly said. "He always comes running when I get home from school."

"He's probably got himself shut in somewhere," said Mom, but she didn't sound as sure as Molly would have liked. She got up and together they went through every room in the house, calling. Every time they opened a door, Molly hoped she'd hear a little patter of paws, and wild yapping, but there was nothing.

No Max.

They went back through every room, more urgently this time, searching under all the beds in case he'd gotten himself stuck, opening the cupboards, Molly frantically calling.

Still nothing.

Back downstairs, Mom was starting to look really worried too. She stood in the living room trying to think back. "I took him in the yard after lunch, but he definitely came back in with me. Then I was working... Oh! Yes, of course, that butterfly surprised him. It flew in through the kitchen window," she explained. "He didn't know what it was. I let it out the window in here..." She did a slow turn toward the window, and her hand went to her mouth in horror. It was still propped open, wide enough for a determined little dog to get out through.

Chapter Three

Meanwhile, Max was trotting along the sidewalk, sniffing enthusiastically. He knew he could find Molly. He'd know her smell anywhere! He had wriggled out of the window quite easily, and fallen into the flower bed, but it didn't matter. Molly was going to be so pleased to see him! Only—he had been expecting to find her by now.

Molly's house was on the edge of the village, and though Max didn't know it, he was going completely the wrong way, heading out of Tilford village and away from the school where Molly had been. He had taken a few turns that looked interesting, passing some more houses like Molly's. Instinctively he'd avoided crossing any roads. The village was very quiet, but a few cars did come past, and he'd been scared. He shrank back against the fences and hedges as he heard them coming, great rushing roaring things that he sensed were dangerous. He stayed hidden against the hedges, and no one saw him. Now he was heading along the road that led to Stambridge, a small town several miles away. It was so nice to be outside, and he trotted along happily for a while, covering a big distance for such a small dog. He would see Molly soon, he was sure.

Eventually he came across an interesting-looking sloping path leading off the sidewalk. It was rough and stony, with sweet-smelling plants on either side. Max plunged down, eager to explore. The path led gently down to a beach, not the main beach where all the vacationers came, but a small rocky cove without much sand that was cut off at high tide. Max stopped short as he got his first sight of the sea. He had no idea what it was. The waves made a swooshing sound as they rushed in and out on the pebbles. He had a feeling that this wasn't where he'd find Molly, but it looked so exciting he had to go and investigate.

He skittered down the rest of the path, scrabbling over the stones, and stood on the beach, sniffing the sharp, salty smell of the sea. He still didn't understand it. It moved, and made a noise—was it alive? He went closer, ears pricked, ready to run if he needed to. With a sudden rush, a wave swept in and soaked his paws. Max yelped and jumped backward. It was cold!

Max stood a little way back from the water and barked angrily at the sea. It didn't seem to be listening, just sweeping in again and hissing at his feet. Max looked at it with his head on one side. Maybe it was playing a game.

Perhaps it wanted him to chase it? He tried, dashing forward as the waves rolled back, then yapping excitedly as it chased him in turn. It was a brilliant game! And the sea didn't get tired and say it needed to sit down for a bit, like Molly and her mom. Max played for a long time.

Then a chilly wind blew up, ruffling the surface of the sea, and Max shivered. Suddenly he realized how hungry he was. In fact, he was starving. Molly would be home by now, and wondering where he was. Max whisked around and scrambled back up the path as quickly as he could. But when he got to the top, he looked around. Which way was home from here? He couldn't remember which way he'd come—he hadn't been thinking about having to go *back*.

Anxiously, Max sniffed the air, hoping to pick up a familiar smell to tell him which way to go. Nothing. No smell of home, or Molly. Max sat down at the top of the path, huddling close to the signpost that said *To the Sea*.

No one was in sight, just empty road stretching out in both directions. Seagulls were crying, but that was the only sound. Max whined miserably. He was lost.

Suddenly a low buzzing sound rose in the distance, quickly getting louder and louder. Max looked around, and cowered back against the signpost as a car shot by, engine roaring, and vanished down the road. He had to

move. He needed to find Molly, and get away from noisy monsters like that. Determinedly, he trotted a few steps down the road. He wasn't sure if it was the right way, but he had to go *somewhere*.

The road seemed to go on an awfully long way. Max was starving—he was used to several small meals of his special puppy food a day, and it felt like he'd missed at least three of them.

As he plodded on, his paws started to hurt too, because he'd never walked so far before. And it was getting harder to see, the daylight slowly disappearing, leaving a strange half-dusk that made shapes loom up at him. All the trees seemed to be waving big, scary branches at him, and the seagulls' cries suddenly sounded eerie.

Max stopped for a rest, hiding in between some clumps of grass at the side of the road. He'd gone a long way out of the village by now, and the road didn't have sidewalks any more, just grassy banks on either side. Things were scurrying in the hedge behind him, and more and more Max wished he'd never left his warm, comfortable, *safe* house behind.

He stood up and pushed on, determined to find his way home. It suddenly seemed to have gotten a lot darker, and Max was so tired and confused that he started to wander along in the middle of the road, his legs shaking with weariness. But he refused to give up.

Another low buzzing noise started; this time he felt it in his paws before he heard it. A car! Max looked around, frightened and confused by the bright lights that were racing up behind him. He tried to get out of the way, but he didn't know which way to go, and he wavered disastrously in its path. The driver didn't even see him.

The car caught him with the edge of its front bumper, and Max was thrown clear, landing in the hedge. He lay unconscious in the long grass, his leg bleeding.

When Molly's dad got home from work, the house was empty, but he could hear Molly's voice calling from the backyard.

"Max! Max, where are you?" Molly sounded upset and her dad dropped his bag in the hall and hurried out to see what was going on.

"Has Max gotten out?" he asked anxiously. "He didn't wriggle under the fence, did he? I thought that gap was too small."

Molly shook her head. Her eyes were

full of tears, and she gave her dad a hug, burying her face in his coat. She didn't want to be the one to tell him.

Molly's mom came down the side path around the house. "Oh, James, you're back!" She was feeling terribly guilty about accidentally letting Max out, and she kept telling Molly how sorry she was. "I left the front window open, and Max got out. We've checked the block, but we can't find him anywhere."

Molly was trying hard to forgive her mom, because she knew she hadn't meant to leave the window open, but it was difficult.

"There's just no sign of him," Mom said, sounding close to tears. "I've spoken to all the neighbors, and no one's seen him. But they've promised to keep a lookout for him."

"If only he'd had his collar on," Molly said miserably. They'd bought Max a collar, but he hadn't been wearing it. He hadn't needed it on when he was only in the house and yard. They'd also been planning to take Max to the vet's to get his next lot of booster vaccinations, and the vet was going to put a microchip in his neck. It would have meant that if he got lost, any vet could check the chip and would know who he belonged to. They'd even made an appointment for it to be done in a few weeks' time. They were taking him to the vet's close to where Mrs. Hughes lived, the one she used for her dogs. It was half an hour's drive away, but Mrs. Hughes said they were really good. The thought made Molly's eyes fill with tears. Who knew where Max would be by then?

That night, Molly went to bed worn out from searching up and down her street, and around the village, and cried herself to sleep. But a hundred miles away, another girl lay awake, too excited to close her eyes. In the corner of Jasmine's bedroom was a small suitcase, already packed, just waiting for her to add her toiletries the next morning. She knew she ought to go to sleep, as they were going to get up at six, and Dad wanted to be on the road by six-thirty, but she just couldn't stop thinking about how exciting it was to be going on vacation. And to the seaside! It was only May, so it wouldn't be hot enough for much sunbathing, but she could swim, and build sand castles, and eat lots and lots of ice cream! It was going to be fantastic.

Jasmine must have fallen asleep eventually, because next thing she knew, her mom was shaking her awake. For once she didn't have to be told to get up quickly; she was downstairs five minutes later.

"I'm too excited for breakfast," said Jasmine, when her mother offered toast.

"You need to eat something, it's going to take us all morning to get there," her dad pointed out. He was drinking a cup of coffee, and having another look at the map. "Right. So we come off the highway, and then once we get to Stambridge, that's the nearest town, we keep going along the cliff road, but we have to make sure we spot the sign for the cottage. The instructions from the vacation cottage people say if we get to Tilford, that's a village about five miles farther on, then we have to turn around because we've missed it! OK, I'm going to go and put these bags in the car." He ruffled Jasmine's hair as he went past. "Don't worry, Jasmine, we'll be on the beach this afternoon!"

Max was still lying huddled under the hedge, his leg throbbing with pain. He felt weak and dizzy, and he couldn't stand up. He was so frightened. What was going to happen to him? Molly had no idea where he was—he didn't even know where he was.

He still wasn't really sure what had happened, either. He'd been wearily wandering along the road, then those enormous lights had swept over him, and something hit him. Then he didn't remember anymore. He wanted Molly. With a sad little snuffling noise, he laid his head down on his front paws. He couldn't move—he'd tried and his leg wasn't working. All he could do was wait, and hope. Maybe Molly would come looking for him. She wouldn't give up on him, would she?

Chapter Four

Jasmine bounced excitedly around the vacation cottage, racing in and out of all the rooms, and getting under Mom and Dad's feet.

"Can we go out and have a look around? Can we go and see the sea?" she kept asking.

"As soon as we've emptied the car, I promise," her mom said, as she unpacked all the food they'd brought and stored it in the cupboards.

Jasmine sighed, and perched herself on the window sill to stare out. The little cottage was right on the cliff, with only a tiny patch of grass separating it from a huge drop to the sea. Mom and Dad had already made her promise faithfully to stay away from the edge. She had a beautiful view out to sea. The sun was sparkling on the water, and a couple of small boats were sailing past. The cottage was just outside a little town called Stambridge. If they walked one way they'd get to the town, which had lots of very interesting-looking shops that Jasmine had spotted on their way through, and if they went the other way they'd reach one of the many little paths down to the beach. Jasmine had been thinking that they should go and investigate the shops first, and maybe buy an ice cream, but the expanse of shining water was calling to her, and now she definitely wanted to find the path down the cliff.

At last her parents had finished the unpacking and they were ready to go and explore.

"Shall we go and get an ice cream?" her dad suggested. "I could use something to cool me down after lugging all those bags around."

"Oh, please can we go and look at the beach first?" Jasmine begged. "And can we go for a swim? The sea looks so lovely out of the window, really blue, with little waves. Pleeeaase!"

"I don't believe it. You're turning down an ice cream?" Jasmine's mom said, laughing.

Jasmine looked thoughtful. "Well, I'm not saying I don't *want* one…"

Her dad grinned. "I'm sure we can do both. Let's go and have a quick look at the sea, and then head into the town to explore."

Eagerly they set off along the road. It had a real country feel, not like the smooth sidewalks Jasmine was used to at home. This road had steep banks, and hedges, full of wild flowers, and every so often something scuttled into the undergrowth as they passed. Just along from the cottage, a little white-painted signpost pointing the other way said *Stambridge 2 miles*. Jasmine walked ahead, looking excitedly for a path down to the sea.

"Oh, look! Here it is!" she called back, waving to her parents to catch up.

All at once, there was a strange little scuffling noise in the grass on the bank, and Jasmine jumped back. "Ugh! I hope it isn't a rat!" she said nervously to herself. But the scuffling was followed by a tiny whimpering sound. That definitely wasn't a rat. It sounded more like a dog...

Max had heard Jasmine calling, and for one hopeful moment he had thought it was Molly come to find him. He quickly realized it wasn't her, this girl didn't smell right, but maybe she would help him anyway. He struggled to get up, but he couldn't, his leg hurt so much, so he just called out to her. *Please! Help me!* he whimpered.

Jasmine crouched down cautiously to peer into the grass, and saw Max's black eyes staring back at her, glazed and dull with pain. He thumped his tail wearily to show he was glad to see her.

"Oh, wow, aren't you gorgeous? What are you doing here, puppy? Are you lost?" Then Jasmine saw his leg and gasped. She jumped up. "Mom! Dad! Come here, quick!"

Her parents had been dawdling along, enjoying the early summer sunshine. Jasmine's anxious voice jerked them out of their daydream.

"What is it?" her dad asked, dashing up.

"It's a dog, a puppy, I mean. He's hurt! Oh, Dad, look at his leg..." Jasmine's voice faltered. Max's leg was badly cut and had bled a lot all over his beautiful white fur. "What are we going to do?"

"He must have been hit by a car," said Dad. "Poor little thing." He turned to Jasmine's mom, who'd come running after them. "Did you see a vet's in Stambridge as we drove through?"

Jasmine's mom shook her head. "I'm not sure, but I should think there would be. Is the little dog hurt?" she asked worriedly.

"Hit by a car, I think. We can't leave him here." He looked down at Max. "I wonder when it happened. He looks pretty weak."

Jasmine's mom nodded. "Look, you and Jasmine stay here, I'll go back and get the car, and some towels or something to wrap him in. Then we can drive him into Stambridge and ask someone about a vet."

"Please be quick, Mom!" Jasmine gulped. The puppy looked so weak and ill lying in the grass. "Do you think it would be OK to pick him up?" she asked her dad. "He looks so sad."

Dad shook his head. "I don't think we should move him more than we have to. His leg might be broken, or he might have other injuries we don't know about. And if he's really hurting, he might snap at you, Jasmine."

Jasmine shook her head. "I'm sure he wouldn't. He looks such a nice little dog."

Max whined again, and stretched his neck to get closer to Jasmine. She wasn't his Molly, but he could tell she was kind and friendly.

Very gently, trying not to frighten him, Jasmine put her hand out for Max to sniff.

Max licked her hand a little, then exhausted by even such a tiny effort, he slumped back.

"Oh, no. I wish Mom would hurry with the car." Jasmine looked around anxiously, then spotted their car coming along the road.

"How's he doing?" her mom asked as she jumped out, grabbing a pile of towels.

Jasmine's eyes were full of tears as she answered. "He's getting weaker. We have to hurry."

The vet's receptionist looked up as they barged through the door. "Oh, I'm sorry, we're actually just about to close—" Then she caught sight of the puppy huddled in a towel in Jasmine's arms, and the blood seeping through the pale pink fabric. "Bring him through! This way. Mike, we've got an emergency," she called as she held open a door for Jasmine and her parents.

A tall, youngish man in a white coat was looking at a computer screen inside the room, which was very clean and shiny, and smelled of disinfectant. He swung around quickly, his eyes going straight to the towel-wrapped bundle.

Jasmine just held Max out to him, not saying anything. She didn't know what to say, and the relief of finally getting to the vet's, where someone might be able to help the poor little dog, was making her feel choked with tears.

The vet took Max and laid him carefully on the table. His eyes were closed, and he wasn't moving. Jasmine knew he was still alive, because she'd been watching him breathing, but even that seemed to have gotten weaker in the last few minutes.

The vet started gently checking Max over. "What happened?" he asked, without looking up.

"We don't know," Jasmine whispered. "We found him."

"We're here on vacation," her dad explained. "We were out for a walk, and Jasmine heard him crying in the hedge. We guessed he'd been hit by a car."

The vet nodded. "He's very lucky. If he'd been out there much longer I don't think he'd have made it. As it is" —he looked up at Jasmine— "I can't promise that he will, but he's got a fighting chance. His leg isn't broken, just badly cut, but he's lost a lot of blood, and he's very weak. I'm going to sedate him and put him on a drip, then stitch up the cut.

If he turns the corner in the next couple of hours, he should be OK. But he's really young, and that amount of blood loss in such a small dog…" He tailed off, but they all knew what he meant.

Jasmine gulped. "Can we wait while you do it? That would be OK, wouldn't it?" she asked her parents.

The vet smiled sympathetically at her. "Of course. You can stay in the waiting room." He was already gently gathering Max up, to take him to the operating room. The puppy looked so small and helpless, and Jasmine just couldn't hold back the tears that were starting to trickle down the side of her nose.

Her mom hugged her gently, and led her out to the waiting room—and that was all they could do, just wait.

When the vet came back out into the reception area he was looking cautiously pleased. Jasmine had been sitting leaning against her mom's shoulder, feeling worn out from her excitement and panic at finding the hurt puppy. But she jumped up immediately. "Is he going to be OK?"

The vet nodded slowly. "I think so. He's certainly got a good chance. The cut on his leg should heal well now it's stitched, and apart from that he's just badly bruised. Definitely no fractures. He really was lucky. He's just sleeping off the anesthetic now." He smiled down at Jasmine. "Would you like to come and see him?"

"Oh, please!" Jasmine nodded, and they followed him through to a room at the back of the surgery that was lined with cages. Most were empty— Jasmine guessed they didn't do that many operations at the weekend—but at one end, by the window, a small black-and-white shape was snuggled into a blue blanket. Jasmine peered in.

The little puppy was fast asleep, but he seemed to be breathing more easily, and the horrible wound on his leg was clean and neatly stitched.

"He should be fine when he wakes up," the vet said hopefully. "He'll be sleepy for the rest of the day, though. He'll have to take some painkillers in his food for a few days, and in a week or so he'll need the stitches out, but that's all. We're not open tomorrow, but I'll be here anyway at about nine if you want to drop in and see how he is."

Jasmine nodded eagerly, and then realized that her mom and dad might not want to. She gave them a pleading sort of look.

Her dad smiled. "It's OK, Jasmine. I'd like to know how he's doing too. Now that we've rescued him, it feels almost like he's ours."

Jasmine smiled wistfully. If only! She would so love to have a dog. But she could never be lucky enough to own a gorgeous puppy like this.

Chapter Five

Vacation was meant to be fun, Molly thought miserably. You weren't supposed to spend all day holed up in your bedroom, because you were too sad even to call and ask a friend over. Molly just didn't think she could face any of her friends at the moment. Max had been missing since Friday, and now it was Monday. Molly wasn't giving up, of course she wasn't, but her frantic searching was starting to seem hopeless. Listlessly, she heaved herself off her bed, and went downstairs to find her mom.

Molly was pretty certain that her mom had given up hope of ever finding Max. She kept gently trying to point out to Molly that there had been no sign of him for three days, and no one had even mentioned seeing a puppy. But she was clearly still feeling so guilty about letting him get out that she agreed to go searching whenever Molly asked. They'd spent at least a couple of hours out looking every day so far, walking around the village, asking people if they'd seen a little black-and-white puppy.

When Molly opened her mom's office door, her mom beckoned her over to the computer. "Look, I've been working on something for you," she said in a pleased voice.

Molly gulped. Max's face was staring at her from the screen, the word LOST shouting out at her. It was one of her favorite photos of him—you could just tell he was wagging his tail like mad, even though it was only his head showing. His tongue was hanging out a bit, and his eyes gazed brightly into hers.

Her mom scrolled down to show her their phone number and a note saying when Max had disappeared, and asking people to check their garages and sheds in case he'd gotten shut in. "I thought we could print them out and put them up all over the village. I know we've asked most people already, but maybe the photo will jog people's memories?"

Molly nodded, still feeling too

choked to speak. It was so awful to think that she might only ever see Max again in photos like this one. She mustn't think like that. But it was getting very hard not to…

"He looks great!" Jasmine gazed delightedly at the puppy frisking around with an old chew-toy on Monday morning. He was totally different from the weak, pitiful little creature he'd been two days before. "His leg seems so much better."

The scary-looking cut was now just a neat line of stitches in a shaved patch of pinkish skin. Even the redness around the stitches seemed to be fading away.

"He does look good, doesn't he? Puppies tend to heal pretty quickly," the vet agreed, smiling down at him. "He's a great character, really cheeky. And he's a pedigreed Old English sheepdog puppy, too, I think. Probably quite valuable."

Jasmine's mom was looking thoughtful. "If he's a pedigree puppy," she said, "he's not likely to have been abandoned, is he? He must have gotten lost. His owners must be really upset."

The vet nodded. "Yes, to be honest, I'm surprised we haven't heard anything. Stambridge isn't that big a place. I would have thought that if anyone had lost a special little dog like this, they'd have let the police know, and it would have been passed on to us too.

He's too young to have been chipped, unfortunately." Seeing Jasmine's blank look, he explained, "Microchipped. A lot of dog owners have a tiny ID chip injected into their dog's neck, just in case something like this happens. It's a really good idea."

"So you haven't heard anything?" Jasmine said slowly, petting the little dog's ears. She supposed she ought to hope that his owners would find him, and he'd soon be back at home and safe, but she just couldn't. She'd been visiting the vet's every day to see how he was—she was more interested in the puppy than in her vacation!

"No, no one's been in touch. There are a couple of other vets in the area, and I've called them, and we're going to put his photo up on our website. I think we're going to have to give him a name—I can't keep on just calling him 'puppy'!"

Jasmine smiled. "I think you should call him Lucky," she said, glad to be distracted from thinking about the puppy's real owners. "You said when we brought him in that he was lucky that the car only just caught him, and that we found him just in time."

The vet nodded. "Mmm, that's a good idea."

The puppy looked up hopefully. He could tell they were talking about him. He liked this nice girl. She'd picked him up and carried him when he was hurt, and she kept coming to see him and play with him.

"Would you like to be called Lucky?" she said, kneeling down next to him. "Lucky? Is that a good name?"

The puppy managed a little jump up to lick her face, and barked gently, to show her he was grateful for all her petting.

"There, he likes it!" Jasmine said delightedly.

And so Max became Lucky...

Jasmine was quiet in the car that afternoon. They were on their way to visit some caves with underground waterfalls that her dad had found a brochure on, but she couldn't seem to feel excited about it.

"Are you all right, Jasmine?" her mom

asked. "The caves should be fun, you know. Lots of interesting stuff to see."

"I know," Jasmine said, forcing a smile.

It didn't work. "You're upset about the puppy, aren't you?" her mom said gently. "But Jasmine, you must have known the vet would try to find his owners. They'll be desperate to find him, and I'm sure he misses them too."

"I suppose," Jasmine muttered. Actually, she couldn't help feeling that whoever had lost Lucky didn't deserve to have him, letting him run off and get hurt.

"It might even be another girl like you, Jasmine," her dad put in. "Imagine if Lucky was yours, and you'd lost him, think how upset you'd be."

"I wouldn't have lost him!" Jasmine

burst out. "Sorry," she sniffed through her tears. "I know we can't have him, but he's so sweet, and I've always wanted a dog, and just finding him like that, it seemed so perfect…"

"And you'd been dreaming of keeping him," her mom sighed. "Oh, Jasmine, I know. He is gorgeous. But he really does belong to someone else. And besides, a dog … it would be such a lot of work…" But she looked thoughtfully at Jasmine's dad as she said it.

Jasmine blew her nose firmly. "Sorry. I'm all right now. Can we go to the caves? Will there be diamonds, or anything?" she said, trying hard to sound enthusiastic. It didn't really work, but Jasmine's dad gave her mom another thoughtful look.

"Molly! Hey, Molly, wait!"

Molly and her mom turned around to see Amy dashing toward her, followed by her big sister Sarah. "Are you going out looking for Max again? We saw you go past and Mom says me and Sarah can come and help if you like."

"If that's OK," Sarah added to Molly's mom.

Molly managed a small smile. It was really sweet of Amy to want to help. "We're putting up these posters," she explained, holding one out.

Amy looked at the photo. "Oh, he looks so cute," she said sadly. "Posters are a really good idea. Are you going to put them up in the supermarket? My gran did that when her cat suddenly went missing, and someone phoned her the next day to say they'd seen him."

"I hadn't thought of putting them in shops, Amy," Molly's mom said. "That's very helpful. I should think most of the shops on the main street would let us."

Molly nodded hopefully. "Yes, then anyone coming in from the vacation cottages along the cliffs to do their shopping would see them."

They shared out rolls of sticky tape and walked quickly along the street, taping the posters onto lampposts and pinning them to fences. Molly kept having to stare into Max's beautiful big eyes as she stuck his picture up all over the village. It was so hard.

Amy put an arm around Molly's shoulders. "Hey," she murmured. "You never know. In a couple of days we'll probably be coming over and taking them all down because we've found him." She smiled at Molly, who wished she could feel so positive.

It was probably just natural puppy healing power that made Lucky's leg get better so quickly, but Jasmine liked to think that his new name had something to do with it. That and all the cuddles, games of hide-the-squeaky-bone, and snoozing on her lap that he'd been having. How could he not get well when everyone loved him so much?

"He really is doing brilliantly," the vet said, shaking his head in amazement as he watched Lucky skidding across the floor after a new toy that Jasmine had brought with her on Wednesday morning, a fluffy knotted rope that had cost a considerable amount of her vacation spending money. "He'll be ready to go soon," the vet added thoughtfully. "I wouldn't have kept him for so long, except that I was hoping his owner might turn up to claim him. No one's called about the photo on our website though."

Jasmine gulped. "Go?" She faltered. "Um, go where?" Without really thinking about it, she snuggled Lucky close into her arms, and he licked her nose happily.

"To the animal shelter. It doesn't look like we're going to have any luck finding his real owner, so poor old Lucky's going to have to find someone new. I'd love to keep him here, but we're so busy. He needs more space and proper looking after, now he's strong enough to move around again."

A shelter! It sounded awful. Jasmine knew that animal shelters did a fantastic job looking after strays and unwanted pets, but she still couldn't help thinking of them as grim, scary places. She didn't want Lucky to have to go to one of those!

"Anyway, it's been fantastic having you here to help look after him," the vet said gratefully. "I don't know what we'd have done without you." He grinned. "I tell you what. It's your last day on Friday, isn't it?"

Jasmine nodded sadly. She didn't want to think about it. She was going to miss seeing Lucky so much!

"Well, to say thank you, how would you like to take Lucky out for his first walk? I reckon his leg will be strong enough by then. You can let him have a walk on the beach. I gave him his puppy booster shots when you first brought him in, so he'd have less chance of picking up anything nasty from any other dogs here. He'll be fine to take out now. We can lend you a leash for him."

"Oh, I'd love to!" Jasmine hugged

Lucky tightly, and looked around at her mom, her eyes shining with excitement. She imagined them wandering along the beach together, Lucky nosing into all the good-smelling holes between the rocks, as she held onto his leash.

It would be just like having her own dog…

Chapter Six

"Look, Lucky! The sea!" Jasmine crouched down beside the puppy, and pointed out over what seemed like miles of perfect sand to the water glinting blue in the sun. "I guess you've *probably* seen it before," she said doubtfully. "Anyway, Mom says that because the tide is out, we can walk along the shore to the next village. And there's a café there that does great milk shakes. Don't worry," she added, stroking his ears, "I'll carry you if you get tired."

Lucky wasn't really listening. He was taking deep, excited sniffs of the salty sea air. It had an unmistakable scent. And the last time he'd smelled it had been the day he lost Molly. Maybe he was close to her again! Wagging his tail briskly, he set off down the cliff path, with Jasmine trotting behind him, and her parents sauntering gently after them.

It was a gorgeous day for a walk, blue sky reflected in blue sea, and the low tide leaving the sand firm and golden and biscuity, and dotted with exciting things for a small dog to investigate.

"Uuurgh, Lucky, no…" Jasmine gently pushed him away from the dead crab he'd found. "It'll make you sick."

Lucky looked up at her reproachfully. But it smelled wonderful!

Jasmine ran after him, laughing, as he darted about, but every so often a small, cold thought would surface. *This is the last time.* They were going home tomorrow, early, and when they took

Lucky back to the vet's later this morning, she would have to say good-bye. Unless, of course… Jasmine just couldn't help feeling that Mom and Dad loved Lucky too. She glanced around, and saw them smiling at Lucky, who was squeaking as a wave came just a bit closer than he'd thought it would. Maybe in just a few more minutes it would be time to ask…

Molly tramped slowly along the beach, a little way behind her mom and dad. Every so often she called for Max, but there was no hope in her voice anymore. She was only doing it because if she didn't, it meant she'd given up, and that meant she was never going to see him again. At least if she was still looking she could tell herself there was a chance.

Her dad had stayed off work today so they could have a long weekend together, and he and Molly's mom had been trying to cheer her up by suggesting a walk along the beach to Stambridge. Usually it was something she loved to do—it was exciting knowing that you were racing the tide, even though there were so many paths up the cliff that it wasn't really dangerous. But today, all Molly could think about was that she'd wanted to do this walk with Max.

Molly sighed miserably. Max would have loved the beach so much. She could imagine him so easily, scuffling through the sand, bouncing at the edge of the water, barking at the seagulls. Just like the little dog she could see way up the beach with another family, dragging a girl her own age along as he chased the waves. A sick, miserable tide of jealousy swept over Molly as she watched them. She blinked tears back from her eyes. The dog even *looked* like her Max.

Molly sniffed determinedly and looked away. "Max! Max!" she called hoarsely. "Here, Max, come on!"

Nothing happened. Molly wiped her arm across her eyes, and marched on after her mom and dad, staring at the stones. Maybe it was time to stop searching. She was just making herself feel worse.

Farther up the beach, Lucky stood listening intently, his black ears tensed. He leaned forward, pulling on his leash, gazing across the sand. There were people walking along the beach, and one of them looked like Molly.

Forgetting that he was on a leash,

and that his leg was still a bit sore, Lucky raced down the beach, barking excitedly, and dragging Jasmine stumbling behind him.

"Jasmine! Are you all right?" her mom called, seeing her fighting to keep up. She and Jasmine's dad hurried after them.

Molly looked up when she heard the barking, and her stomach twisted miserably. The puppy sounded just like Max too. In fact… Molly narrowed her eyes, and stared. It looked like Max because that *was* Max, hurling himself down the beach toward her, towing that girl.

Molly started to run, overtaking her mom and dad.

Max raced toward her even faster, desperate in case he lost her again. In a flurry of fur and sand, he flung himself at her, barking and wagging his tail and climbing into her lap as she knelt down to hug him.

"Max! You came back! Oh, where have you been? I can't believe I've found you again!" Molly gasped into his fur.

Max gave an overjoyed woof and licked the tears off her face.

"His name's Lucky," a small voice said sadly.

Molly suddenly remembered that Max was wearing a leash, and somebody else was on the other end of it. She looked up, to see a blond, curly-haired girl staring down at Max.

"Or that's what we called him, anyway," the girl said, and sniffed. "I suppose he's yours, isn't he…?"

She looked like she was trying really hard not to cry, and Molly stood up slowly, cuddling Max close. "Um, yes. He climbed out the window. Exactly a week ago. My mom left it open and he got out and we've been looking for him ever since."

"Oh." Jasmine nodded. That explained it then. "He got hit by a car," she told Lucky's real owner. "We found him. We're here on vacation."

Molly gasped in horror. "Hit by a car! Is he OK?"

Jasmine showed Molly the cut on Max's leg. "He was really lucky. The car just nicked his leg, but it's healing really well. I've been visiting him every day." She sniffed, again, and a tear rolled down her cheek. "I'm glad you've got him back, because he looks happy being back with you ... but I really wish we'd walked along the beach the other way!" And she turned and started stumbling away, feeling as though she couldn't bear to watch that other girl cuddling Lucky, *owning* him.

"Hey!" Molly called after her, but by this time both sets of parents had come hurrying up, and Jasmine's mom had caught her and was holding her tight.

Molly watched her hiding her face in her mom's jacket, as everyone tried to explain what was going on all at once. Jasmine's mom took her to sit on a rock a little way away from the others, and found some tissues, and her dad told Molly and her parents about how they'd found Max.

"We really can't thank you enough," Molly's dad said, shaking his head. "Max could have died."

"It was just so lucky Jasmine found him," Molly's mom said, stroking Max's head gently. "I can't believe we've got him back."

Jasmine's dad smiled. "He's a great little dog. I have to tell you, we'd pretty much decided that we were going to keep him." He looked over at Jasmine. "Jasmine doesn't know that. She looked after him so well. I think we'll have to give her a while to stop missing him, but then we'll think about getting a puppy of our own."

"Oh!" Molly gasped as a brilliant idea hit her. "Mom! Jasmine could have Max's brother!"

"Oh, Molly, I'm not sure..." her mom said doubtfully.

"There's another boy puppy in the litter Max came from," Molly explained to Jasmine's dad. "Couldn't we take them to see him?" she begged her parents. "I bet Jasmine would love him. He really looks like Max."

Jasmine's dad looked thoughtfully over at her and her mom. "I don't know. I suppose we could see." He walked toward them. "Jasmine, listen, we've had an idea..."

Jasmine stood in Mrs. Hughes's kitchen, feeling totally miserable, and trying not to show it. She ought to be really excited. Lucky (she still couldn't get her head around calling him Max) had found his real owners again, and wouldn't have to go to a shelter. *And* her mom and dad had just told her that even though they couldn't keep Lucky, they did want to get a dog, and Lucky's brother was for sale. But it was like everyone was expecting her to adore this strange puppy straight away, after she'd spent a week falling in love with Lucky.

Lucky had been left in Molly's parents' car with Molly's dad, because it might confuse him to see his brother and sisters again. The three puppies who hadn't gone to new homes yet were playing with a squidgy ball, romping all over their mom and dad, who were huge. Jasmine could see why

Molly had thought of her plan—one of the puppies did look almost exactly like Lucky.

"So what do you think, Jasmine?" her mom asked anxiously.

"Um…" Jasmine didn't know what to say. It was so awful. Molly and her parents were trying to be kind, and she felt really guilty. Trying to hide how she felt, Jasmine knelt down to play with the puppies, although she didn't really want to. They looked at her inquisitively, their bright eyes questioning, their ears pricking up. Jasmine couldn't help smiling a little. They were so sweet.

The boy puppy with Lucky's same pirate eyepatch gave a little bark. It was so clearly an invitation, or possibly even an order—*play with me!*

Jasmine giggled at the bossy little dog, and rolled the ball toward him. He yapped delightedly and pounced, flinging his paws out to make a grab for it before his sisters did.

Unfortunately, the ball rolled away and he landed on his nose. He sat up and whined, not really that hurt, but embarrassed and a bit annoyed.

"Aww…" Jasmine picked him up and cuddled him.

The puppy snuggled into her arms, the ball forgotten as he enjoyed being cuddled. He nuzzled his nose under her chin lovingly, and Jasmine laughed as his cold, wet nose brushed her ear.

Then a sharp, shocking memory of Lucky doing just the same thing made Jasmine put the puppy down suddenly. Surprised, he whined, clearly wanting more petting, his big dark eyes pleading. "Sorry, little one," Jasmine murmured, rubbing him behind the ears. "I didn't mean to do that. I just…"

The puppy clambered into her lap
and licked her cheek forgivingly. His
tongue managed to be soft and rough at
the same time, and Jasmine wriggled
and laughed. He was tickling! Suddenly
something inside her that had frozen
up when Lucky raced away from her on
the beach melted, and she gave
Lucky's brother a big hug.
Holding him tight, she
stood up carefully,
and looked around
at her parents.

"Do you think
we could call
him Lucky
too?"